11/17

07 NOV 2023

DEA

Books should be returned or renewed by the last date above. Renew by phone 03000 41 31 31 or online *www.kent.gov.uk/libs*

'Saunde... ...e likely to make you laugh
in publi... ...This is an important book'
Nation...

D1407168

Praise for George Saunders

'Not since Twain has America produced a satirist this funny' Zadie Smith

'Again and again, Saunders demonstrates that wacky, subversive, formally strange writing is not only contrary to our nation's capitalist spirit, it's the most natural and effective of responses to it. He makes the all-but-impossible look effortless' Jonathan Franzen

'Is this satire? Not quite. Sci-fi? Almost. Whatever, it can often be dark, concerned, confused and funny, all at the same time ... Like so much of Saunders', brilliant, crazy writing it's relevant, but not too relevant' The Times

'You do not read Saunders' stories so much as watch them detonate on the page in front of you, like a firecracker some joker has slipped into your pudding' Stephen Amidon, New Statesman

'Reading George Saunders is, it's safe to say, like no other literary experience ... Surreal, rather moving and deeply angry' Observer

'Saunders, as an American social and literary critic, may be shaping up as the Orwell of the millennium' The Times

'A sense of humour half-way between Beckett and Monty Python ... An anarchic satirist' Sunday Telegraph

'Saunders' jabs are sharp and scary, but also sad and unexpectedly touching' Guardian

'Saunders' writing recognisably emerges from a literary apprenticeship that he shares with writers such as Wallace, Eggers and Foer ... These are dark, funny stories, but they are also infused with compassion' TLS

'Saunders' true strength is comic creativity, the wit and ingenuity that go into designing his pseudo-worlds' Literary Review

'Saunders can capture the absurdity of our condition far more uproariously than a hundred "humorous" guides to modern life' Daily Mail

'Painfully funny ... The man is alarmingly good' Evening Standard

'Saunders' novella is as savagely witty and slightly demented as we have come to expect from this brilliant satirist' Metro

'...ers is the funniest writer in American, more...
...ne than any other writer since P.G. Wodehouse ...'

George Saunders is the author of nine books, including *Tenth of December*, which was a finalist for the National Book Award and won the inaugural Folio Prize (for the best work of fiction in English) and the Story Prize (best short-story collection). He has received MacArthur and Guggenheim fellowships and the PEN/Malamud Prize for excellence in the short story, and was recently elected to the American Academy of Arts and Sciences. In 2013, he was named one of the world's 100 most influential people by *Time* magazine. He teaches in the creative writing program at Syracuse University.

georgesaundersbooks.com

By George Saunders

FICTION

CivilWarLand in Bad Decline
Pastoralia
The Very Persistent Gappers of Frip
The Brief and Frightening Reign of Phil
In Persuasion Nation
Tenth of December
Lincoln in the Bardo

NONFICTION

The Brain-Dead Megaphone
Congratulations, By the Way

GEORGE
SAUNDERS

THE BRIEF AND
FRIGHTENING
REIGN
OF PHIL

BLOOMSBURY
LONDON · OXFORD · NEW YORK · NEW DELHI · SYDNEY

Bloomsbury Paperbacks
An imprint of Bloomsbury Publishing Plc

50 Bedford Square
London
WC1B 3DP
UK

1385 Broadway
New York
NY 10018
USA

www.bloomsbury.com

BLOOMSBURY and the Diana logo are trademarks of Bloomsbury Publishing Plc

First published in Great Britain 2006
This paperback edition first published in 2017

British Library Cataloguing-in-Publication Data
A catalogue record for this book is available from the British Library.

ISBN: PB: 978-1-4088-7052-5
        ePub: 978-1-4088-2253-1

2 4 6 8 10 9 7 5 3 1

Typeset by Newgen Knowledge Works Pvt. Ltd., Chennai, India
Printed and bound in Great Britain by CPI Group (UK) Ltd, Croydon CR0 4YY

MIX
Paper from
responsible sources
FSC® C020471

To find out more about our authors and books visit www.bloomsbury.com.
Here you will find extracts, author interviews, details of forthcoming events and
the option to sign up for our newsletters.

To Joe and Sheri Lindbloom,
brilliant teachers, beautiful friends.

It's one thing to be a small country, but the country of Inner Horner was so small only one Inner Hornerite at a time could fit inside, and the other six Inner Hornerites had to wait their turns to live in their own country while standing very timidly in the surrounding country of Outer Horner.

Whenever the Outer Hornerites looked at the hangdog Inner Hornerites crammed into the Short-Term Residency Zone, they felt a little sick, and also very patriotic. Inner Hornerites were pathetic and whiny and grasping, unlike them, the Outer Hornerites, who for many years had been demonstrating their tremendous generosity by allowing the Inner Hornerites to overflow into the Short-Term Residency Zone. Not that the Inner Hornerites appreciated it. No, they never wept with gratitude anymore, only stood very close together, glaring resentfully at the Outer Hornerites, who, having so much room, had no need to stand close together, and in fact could often be seen drinking coffee at the spacious Outer Horner Cafe with their legs thrown out in the aisles, causing the Inner

Hornerites to wonder: Jeez, couldn't those jerks spare us a couple hundred extra square yards of that vast unlimited country?

For their part, the Outer Hornerites felt that, yes, okay, their country was big, but it wasn't infinitely big, which meant they might someday conceivably run out of room. Besides, what if they gave more of their beloved country to Inner Horner and some other crummy little countries came around demanding bits of Outer Horner? What would happen to the Outer Horner way of life, which was so comfortable and afforded them such super dignity and required so much space? Well, those Inner Hornerites could take a flying leap if they considered Outer Hornerites selfish, it was pretty nervy to call someone selfish while standing on land they were letting you use for free.

So it went, year after year, with much mutual glowering and many murmured rude comments and the occasional angry word hissed across the border.

Then one day Inner Horner got smaller. It happened without warning; there was a loud scraping rock-on-rock sound and suddenly three-quarters of Elmer, the Inner Hornerite then in residence, was not in Inner Horner at all. That is, every part of Elmer but the octagonal shovel-like receptacle with which he scooped dirt when nervous was suddenly now located in Outer Horner.

Just then Leon, the Outer Horner Border Guard, came by on his rounds, noted the presence of three-quarters of Elmer in Outer Horner, and rang the loud buzzer that meant Invasion in Progress.

The Outer Horner Militia (Freeda, Melvin, and Larry) came rushing over and stood glaring fiercely across the green piece of string that constituted the boundary of the Short-Term Residency Zone.

"What are you people trying to pull?" said Larry. "What's that part of a guy doing in our country?"

"Our country shrunk," said Elmer, digging nervously in the dirt with his octagonal shovel-like receptacle.

"Oh please," said Freeda. "You expect us to believe that? Our country never shrinks."

"Decent countries don't shrink," said Melvin. "They either stay the same or get bigger."

"Take a look," said Elmer.

And the Outer Horner Militia (Freeda, Melvin, and Larry) looked into the deep heart of Inner Horner, by leaning over the red string that constituted the Inner Horner border, and saw that Inner Horner had, in fact, shrunk.

"Weird," said Melvin.

"Gross," said Larry.

"What do we do now?" said Freeda.

"I say we expulse the invaders," said Larry.

"That sounds pretty good," said Melvin. "How do we?"

"We just, ah, you know, expulse them," said Larry. "Watch. Something like this."

And Larry expulsed Elmer. That is, he pushed the portion of Elmer that was in Outer Horner back into Inner Horner. But since Inner Horner was now too small to accommodate all of Elmer, as the portion of Elmer in Outer Horner was expulsed into Inner Horner, a different portion of Elmer reemerged out of Inner Horner, sort of inadvertently reinvading Outer Horner.

"They're a scrappy, stubborn people," said Melvin. "You've got to give them that."

"Sneaky," said Larry. "That's what they are."

"What you need to do," said someone, with great authority, from over by the Cafe, "is tax them."

This was Phil, a middle-aged Outer Hornerite generally considered a slightly bitter nobody. Many years before, Phil had, from across the border, fallen in love with a largely vertical, left-trending Inner Hornerite named Carol. He was captivated by her glossy black filaments and transparent oscillating membranes, the delicate curve of her exposed spine, her habit of demurely scratching one bearing with a furry glovelike appendage, and spent many hours casually circling Inner Horner, hoping to catch her eye, inflating and deflating his central bladder in order to look more manly and attractive. But no. Carol was in love with Cal, an Inner Hornerite who resembled a gigantic belt buckle with a blue dot affixed to it, if a gigantic belt buckle with a blue dot affixed to it had been stapled to a tuna fish can.

The day of the wedding was the worst of Phil's life.

He stood across the border, heartbroken, passing bits of machine oil from his lower strata as the Inner Hornerites performed their marriage ritual, which consisted of standing even more closely together than usual and singing sentimental songs about the enviable compactness of their country.

Over the years Phil's bitterness increased, as day after day he watched Carol polishing Cal's belt buckle and playfully opening and closing Cal's tuna fish can. When Carol and Cal's son, Little Andy, was born, Phil's bitterness was complete. He couldn't help thinking that, if only Carol had used better judgment and shown better taste, Little Andy could've been his son. Although if Little Andy had been his son, Little Andy would no doubt have been better-looking and more intelligent and certainly wouldn't have been given a dopey Inner Horner–sounding name like Little Andy.

"You tax them," Phil said again. "You charge them for every day they take up room in our beloved land."

"Wow, great idea," said Larry. "How much do we charge?"

"How much do they have?" said Phil.

"How much do you have?" Larry asked the Inner Hornerites.

Using his octagonal shovel-like receptacle, Elmer opened the cash box, which occupied the entire northwest region of Inner Horner.

"Four smolokas," he said.

"Then tax them four," said Phil.

"But then we'll have zero," said Cal.

"Tax them four," said Phil. "They pay us four, they can stay in the Short-Term Residency Zone the rest of the day. That's how you do it. That's fair."

"Pretty smart guy," said Larry.

"Yeah, who knew?" said Melvin.

Now, in addition to having been jilted by the love of his life, Phil had another problem, which was that the bolt holding his brain in position on his tremendous sliding rack occasionally fell out, causing his brain to slide rapidly down his rack and smash into the ground. This happened now. His brain slid down, smashed into the ground, popped off his rack, and rolled into a ditch.

"I'll tell you something else about which I've been lately thinking!" he bellowed in a suddenly stentorian voice. "I've been thinking about our beautiful country! Who gave it to us? I've been thinking about how God the Almighty gave us this beautiful sprawling land as a reward

6

for how wonderful we are. We're big, we're energetic, we're generous, which is reflected in all our myths, which are so very populated with large high-energy folks who give away all they have! If we have a National Virtue, it is that we are generous, if we have a National Defect, it is that we are *too* generous! Is it our fault that these little jerks have such a small crappy land? I think not! God Almighty gave them that small crappy land for reasons of His own. It is not my place to start cross-examining God Almighty, asking why He gave them such a small crappy land, my place is to simply enjoy and protect the big bountiful land God Almighty gave us!"

Suddenly Phil didn't seem like quite so much of a nobody to the other Outer Hornerites. What kind of nobody was so vehement, and used so many confusing phrases with so much certainty, and was so completely accurate about how wonderful and generous and underappreciated they were?

"Boy oh boy," said Freeda.

"He just comes right out and says it," said Melvin.

"Thank goodness someone finally has," said Larry.

"As for you Inner Hornerites!" bellowed Phil. "Please take heed: You are hereby testing the limits of our legendary generosity, because of how you are, which is so very the opposite of us. Friends, take a look at these losers! If they are as good as us, why do they look so much worse

7

than us? Look how they look! Do they look valorous and noble and huge like us, or do they look sad and weak and puny?"

The truth was, long years of timidly standing very close together in the Short-Term Residency Zone whispering complicated mathematical proofs to pass the time had made the Inner Hornerites frail and small, whereas the Outer Hornerites, with an entire huge country to roam around in, were stocky and hearty, and knew absolutely no mathematical proofs.

"Pretty darn puny," said Melvin.

"I never really noticed that before," said Leon the Border Guard.

"Collect the taxes!" shouted Phil, and Freeda reached over the border and seized the Inner Horner cash box.

Larry and Melvin rushed into the ditch, retrieved Phil's brain, and remounted it on his big sliding rack.

"Thank you, my friends," said Phil, his voice suddenly less stentorian. "What wonderful examples of our famous Outer Horner generosity."

Larry gave Melvin a proud secret look, and Melvin gave Larry a proud secret look, and Freeda, counting the contents of the cash box to verify that there were in fact four smolokas inside, felt a little sad that Phil had not cited her as a wonderful example of that famous Outer Horner generosity, and resolved that, next time Phil's brain slid off his rack, she would be the one to remount it.

Next morning, Phil and the Outer Horner Militia (Freeda, Melvin, and Larry) arrived at the border before dawn and stood watching the Inner Hornerites sleep while standing up.

"Snooze, snooze, snooze," said Phil. "Sort of lazy, aren't they?"

"Whereas us," said Larry, "we're up before dawn, diligently working."

"That's right Larry," said Phil. "Good observation."

"Doing our diligent work of collecting taxes," said Melvin.

"Super, Melvin," said Phil. "We really are a diligent people."

"Diligently collecting taxes to protect the security of our nation," said Freeda.

"You know what?" said Phil. "After spending some time with you folks, I am tempted, in terms of our most important National Virtue, to replace 'Generosity' with 'Remarkable Intelligence.'"

Larry, Melvin, and Freeda beamed.

"Now what do you say we collect some taxes?" Phil said,

and nudged Leon, who, with his Border Guard pole, gave Wanda, the nearest Inner Hornerite, a hard poke in her thermal venting apparatus.

The Inner Hornerites woke and, as on every other morning, briefly considered stretching, then remembered that, if they all stretched at once, someone would get knocked out of the Short-Term Residency Zone and would technically be invading Outer Horner.

So they began stretching, one at a time, by age, oldest first.

"Tax time, slackers," said Phil. "Stop that stupid stretching and listen up. You're late with your dang taxes."

"But we don't have any money," said Elmer. "You know we don't. You took it all yesterday."

"Oh, you people," said Phil. "What did you have in mind? Living in our beloved country for free forever? Do you know what we do? In our country? We work. We believe that time is money. Therefore, as time passes, in our land, we diligently work, which produces, guess what? Wealth. Money. Smolokas! You people! Knowing you owed us money, what did you do? You slept all night like babies! Dreaming, probably, of further taking us to the cleaners! So here you are, smolokaless, again owing your daily taxes. What else do you have? Larry, inventory their resources."

Larry looked at Phil blankly.

"Count their stuff," said Phil.

"Oh," said Larry, and inventoried the resources of the nation of Inner Horner, by examining the length and breadth of Inner Horner and carefully recording the results of his inventory on a piece of paper, which he then handed to Phil.

"Okay, let's see," said Phil. "Apple tree, very small: one. Stream, nearly dry: one. Dry cracked dirt: approximately three cubic feet. Excellent, Larry, an excellent inventory. Now, let's assess the total value of their national resources. Freeda, what do you say? Do you say four? Do you say all that junk is worth exactly four smolokas?"

Overnight, Freeda, a lonely bushlike widow, had developed a bit of a crush on authoritative, gleaming, shouting Phil, and nodded her head yes with a rapt look on her face, without even looking at the tree, the stream, or the dirt.

"Excellent job, Freeda," said Phil. "A really nice assessment. Leon: Uproot that tree and drain that stream and dig up that dirt and let's bring it all back home, to Outer Horner."

Leon stepped over the border and uprooted the apple tree and drained the stream into his see-through stomach. Then, using his spadelike tail, he dug up the dirt and added it to the stream in his stomach, making a pale red mud.

"But what will we eat?" said Carol. "What will we drink? What do you expect us to do when it's our turn to live in our country, stand in that hole?"

"That's not really my problem," said Phil. "My problem is, where am I going to store this junky tree and this boring little stream and this laughable dirt? Any suggestions?"

"How about West Distant Outer Horner?" said Larry. "It's pretty empty out there."

"Super input, Larry," said Phil. "Leon, would you do the honors?"

Carrying the tree over his shoulder and the streamwater-dirt mix in his stomach, Leon walked out to West Distant Outer Horner, a bleak area of recurring icy crevasses, and dropped the former national resources of Inner Horner into the deepest, iciest crevasse he could find.

That night in the Short-Term Residency Zone the Inner Hornerites held a whispered frantic national referendum. Years of standing with their limbs intermingled had made the Inner Hornerites extremely considerate of one another's feelings, so much so that even the simplest decision, such as whether to declare it National Bedtime, sometimes took hours.

"So how should we start?" said Elmer. "How should we proceed? What's our primary issue here?"

"Wait a minute, Elmer," said Wanda. "Aren't you getting a little ahead of things? Don't you think we should first determine if determining our primary issue is indeed our highest priority?"

"Which I suppose raises the question of whether determining our highest priority really is in fact our initial goal," said Old Gus, the oldest Inner Hornerite, who was so old and tired he was shaped something like the letter *C*, if the letter *C* was bald and had two gray withered antlers.

"I think the primary issue is, we don't have any food," said Carol.

"I agree with Carol," said Cal, who, after ten years of marriage, was still nuts about Carol.

"Although the lack of water isn't so great either," said Curtis.

"Of course we also have no dirt," said Elmer.

"Well, the lack of dirt I think is not so primary," said Curtis.

"I beg to differ," said Elmer. "I think the lack of dirt is very primary. I mean, look at our country."

And everyone looked at Inner Horner, which now looked something like an open grave.

"To be frank, I'm feeling a little left out of this discussion," said Old Gus. "My concern about whether determining our highest priority was indeed our initial goal appears to have been dismissed out of hand."

Just then Inner Horner was hit with a blinding light

from somewhere up high.

"Phil's orders, folks," said Leon the Border Guard, standing behind a spotlight he had just installed on top of his Guard Shack. "He wants me to keep a better eye on you people, because you're so sneaky, which he feels will be easier if it's not so dark at night."

"Gosh, that's bright," said Wanda.

"Leon, if we're so sneaky, how come you're always playing checkers with us?" said Cal.

"I'm not," said Leon. "I've discontinued that."

"Maybe we should draft a petition of protest," said Wanda. "After first discussing the idea among ourselves, of course."

"Maybe we should hold a straw poll to assess the level of support for the idea of drafting a petition of protest," said Cal.

"I say enough talking," said Curtis. "I say it's time we *did* something."

"Maybe we should go on a hunger strike," said Old Gus.

"Excuse me, Gus," said Carol. "Not to dismiss your idea? But aren't we sort of already on a hunger strike? Because no food? Remember, they took our apple tree? So I'm not sure how effective a hunger strike would be. I mean, they might not even notice we were on one."

"They've essentially put us on one," said Cal.

"I have an idea," said Little Andy.

Even though Little Andy was the youngest Inner Hornerite, he had an acute probing intelligence that the Inner Hornerites all respected, an intelligence probably related to the fact that he had two distinct functional brains, one on the side of his neck and the other on his hip, with a shiny yellow Decider located midway between them.

"Go ahead, son," said Cal.

"Why don't we write a letter to their President?" Little Andy said.

"Ha ha!" said Curtis. "That is so cute."

"That is cute," said Wanda. "But also it's not bad."

Actually it was good. The President of Outer Horner was an affable old man with five white mustaches and seven ample bellies, who many years before, while a student, had spent a semester abroad in Inner Horner, or at least part of him had, and so the conventional wisdom was that he had a soft spot for Inner Horner and Inner Hornerites.

So the Inner Hornerites, with virtually no debate or discussion, blinking in the blinding light, wrote a letter to the President of Outer Horner.

Dear Mr. President, the letter read. *We respectfully request that you bring your honorable several mustaches and historically righteous bellies to the border so we can discuss some taxes that have recently been levied against us by some guy named Phil who, to our knowledge, has nothing to do with your government, or at least we hope not.*

"This will work," said Elmer. "I feel confident this will work."

"The President won't stand for this," said Carol.

Wanda tiptoed out of the Short-Term Residency Zone, into Outer Horner, past the now-sleeping Leon, and slipped the letter into a mailbox outside the Outer Horner Cafe.

Then, ignoring the other Inner Hornerites, who were frantically gesturing for her to hurry home, she stood a few minutes in Outer Horner, extending her tendrils and breathing deep and walking around in wide leisurely circles.

Next afternoon, amid a tremendous fanfare of trumpets and crashing cymbals, the President of Outer Horner arrived at the Border Area, on a lavish Presidential Board carried by a team of sweating, panting Advisors. The President was a small but impressive man consisting of a jumble of bellies, white mustaches, military medals, and dignified double chins, all borne magnificently aloft on three thin wobbly legs.

"Ah, the memories," he said, gazing down into Inner Horner. "Ah, the days of my Youth. It looks quite different than I remember it, of course. Because I was looking at it through the eyes of Youth back then, whereas now I am looking at it through the eyes of Old Age. Have I said that? Lately I'm always repeating myself. It looks quite different than I remember it, of course. I remember apple trees and rushing streams. But of course I was a young buck then, in love with life, with fewer chins and bigger dreams, whereas now I'm an old fossil with my best years behind me, and several additional chins before me, and as for dreams, my only dream is to lose a few of these chins. Ha ha! One must keep one's sense of humor, yes? One must keep one's chins up! Ha ha! Strange how one's memory plays tricks though! I clearly remember apple trees and a rushing stream. And a girl named Mona. Have I said that? Have I already asked if I've already said that, that thing about Mona? I seem to re-member sitting with Mona under an apple tree, beside a rushing stream, under a lush full moon, and also some fond whispered words? Where is Mona? Was there ever a Mona, or did I make that up?"

"There was, sir," said Elmer. "She died just last year."

It was true. Mona had died last year and been buried in the portion of Inner Horner displaced when Inner Horner shrunk, so that, as they spoke, Mona was lying directly be-neath the President.

"Oh dear," the President said. "Mona dead? It seems that only yesterday she was a little cutie, kissing my then-blond mustaches, and now look at me, all white-haired and forgetful and fat, and look at her, all dead and so forth! My advice to you is: Don't get old! Have I said that? Remain young! Because once you get old you start misremembering, for example, that there were apple trees and rushing streams in your youth, when in fact the country where you spent your semester abroad was only a deep ugly gash in the earth."

"Actually, sir," said Cal, "even yesterday we had an apple tree and a stream."

"What's that?" said the President, looking confused. "Then I should've come yesterday, yes? Is that what you're saying? And Mona? Was Mona here yesterday too? Did Mona die just this morning, and I therefore barely missed her, and therefore, had I come only a few hours sooner, she could've stroked my mustaches one last time?"

"Sir," said Cal, "it was Phil who did this. Phil took our tree and our stream."

"Was it Phil who took Mona?" said the President. "Who is this Phil anyway? Is Mona being kept with your tree and your stream, by this Phil character? I wish you'd make yourselves clear. I'm not so young anymore. First you say she's dead, and then you say she's with the stream and the tree, being held hostage by this Phil fellow."

"Sir," said Cal, "Mona's dead."

"I understand that perfectly well!" thundered the President. "I'm not stupid, you know, just forgetful and shaky and cantankerous. I understand everything you've said to me. Mona is dead, killed by Phil, who then stole your tree and stream and moon, the rascal, although how the moon came to be your property, I'm not quite sure. You people are certainly proprietary. The moon, I believe, is for us all. Haven't I often said that?"

"You have, sir," said a Presidential Advisor whose face was a mirror with two shifty eyes set in it. "You have often said that the moon and the stars are for us all."

"And the stars, yes," said the President. "I forgot about the stars being for us all. Write that down. For my next speech. Moon, stars, for us all. That's good."

Just then Phil came clanking up, accompanied by the Outer Horner Militia.

"Mr. President," said Phil. "I beg your pardon, but these people are slandering me."

"Who are you?" said the President.

"I'm Phil, sir," said Phil.

"I don't see why you had to kill Mona, Phil," said the President sadly. "She was a lovely girl."

"I didn't kill anyone," said Phil.

"He didn't kill anyone," said Elmer. "Mona just died on her own."

"For the love of God, man!" the President shouted at Elmer. "Then why claim such a thing? Why accuse an innocent man of murder? That is a very serious accusation.

That's one thing I remember about you people, from my youth, you were always quite frivolous. Take Mona, for example, she was quite frivolous, kissing me like that, and me a stranger, and a foreigner. Kiss kiss kiss, like some sort of crazy woman. So frivolous. Not that I minded! No, I liked it, Mona's frivolousness, it was the best part about her. But this level of frivolousness is something altogether different. Kissing my mustaches is one thing, but falsely accusing Phil of murder, even Mona wasn't frivolous enough to do that, and believe me, she was plenty frivolous. Now tell the truth: Having established that Phil did not kill Mona, did he or did he not do the other things you slandered him with, that is, steal your tree and stream and moon?"

"Just the stream and the tree," said Wanda.

"So you retract your accusation regarding the moon?" said the President disgustedly. "So frivolous. I don't know what to believe anymore."

"Sir, with all due respect," said Phil. "I did take the stream and the tree, but I was only attempting to enforce your decree."

"I'm glad to see someone enforcing my decrees," said the President. "Back in the capital they're always ignoring my decrees. Tell me, which decree were you enforcing? Was it a good decree?"

"The Short-Term Residency Zone Tax Decree," said Phil. "A very good decree."

"I don't remember that one," the President said to his Advisors. "It sounds like a good one but I don't remember it. Did I decree that?"

"Well, sir, it depends," said the mirror-faced Advisor. "What we need to ask ourselves is, what, in general, has been the reaction to this Tax? Have the people been in favor of the Tax? If so, then it is my recollection that you did indeed make such a decree. On the other hand, if the people have been unhappy with this Tax, then I very clearly remember you pounding the table, denouncing someone for even suggesting that you make such a lame-brained decree. It is clear, sir, that we must, to honor our democracy, go to the people, in order to determine just what it is you decreed."

"So be it," said the President grandly. "Let us see what I said."

The Advisors rushed around polling every Outer Hornerite they could find. That is, they polled the Outer Horner Militia (Freeda, Melvin, and Larry) and Leon the Border Guard and Phil himself.

When the votes were counted, it was determined that the people of Outer Horner were unanimous in their support of the Short-Term Residency Zone Tax.

"You know, sir, in light of that vote, I just remembered something," said the Advisor. "You did indeed decree that. It was a Thursday. You decreed the Short-Term Residency

Zone Tax, and I remember I congratulated you, and then you thanked me for helping you come up with that decree. For sort of laying the conceptual groundwork."

"Well, I thank you again," said the President. "Because look how popular you have made me with my people. They look so happy. They look as if they're about to burst into applause."

And Phil and Leon and the Outer Horner Militia burst into applause.

"Mr. President," Phil said when the applause had died down. "May I also just say how proud I am to have been appointed your Special Border Activities Coordinator?"

"Well of course you're proud," said the President. "Who wouldn't be? That's an important job. And I'm glad I appointed you that. If in fact I did. Did I? Did I do that in conjunction with that decree about that Tax thingie?"

"May I suggest we go to the people again?" said the Advisor.

"By all means," said the President, still very much moved by the standing ovation he had recently received.

So once again Freeda, Melvin, Larry, Leon the Border Guard, and Phil himself were polled, and it was determined that the people of Outer Horner were unanimously pleased with the idea of Phil being Special Border Activities Coordinator, and so it was determined, by the President's Advisors, that the President had, in fact, several months ago, appointed Phil to that post, and there was some concern, among the Advisors, that Phil did not appear at present to be wearing his Presidential Appointment Medal. Fortunately an extra was found, hanging over the awning of the youngest Advisor's exposed spleen, and Phil bent low, and the President hung the Presidential Appointment Medal around Phil's neck.

"Now as for you people," the President said sternly to the Inner Hornerites. "I suggest that, in the future, you refrain from all frivolity and false accusations and obey Phil, who has already done so much for you, and will, I'm sure, continue to do so much for you, including, perhaps, someday, if you remain nonfrivolous, obtaining some replacement trees and a replacement stream, to replace those you so frivolously lost."

"Thank you, sir," said Phil.

"No, thank you, Phil," said the President. "For doing such a tremendous job of enforcing my decrees and calling me out here to see what a tremendous job of enforcing my decrees you've been doing. It does me good to see a young man enforcing my decrees. Sort of a protégé!"

Then the Advisors loaded the President back on to the Presidential Board and, straining under the weight, set off for the capital.

"Goodbye, Phil, dear boy!" the President shouted. "Keep up the good work!"

Next morning Phil and the Outer Horner Militia arrived at the border to find the entire population of Inner Horner heaped up in a tremendous teetering pile of grimaces and side-paddles and Thrumton Specialty Valves and cowlicks and rear ends and receding hairlines, a pile that began in the hole that was formerly Inner Horner and rose some thirty feet in the air, leaning precariously out over Outer Horner.

"My God, look at those people," said Melvin.

"So uncouth," said Larry.

"Animals," said Melvin. "How do they live with themselves?"

"I mean, look at us," said Freeda. "You don't see us piling on like that."

"They seem sort of imprisoned by their own dark urges," said Larry.

Everyone looked at Larry, impressed.

"No wonder we treat them so unfairly," said Melvin, trying to counter Larry.

"Not that we treat them unfairly, Melvin," said Phil a little sternly.

"Oh, we treat them fairly," said Melvin. "I'm just saying, you know, think how fairly we'd treat them if they didn't behave like uncouth animals imprisoned by their dark surges."

"Urges," corrected Larry.

"What are you schmoes doing up there anyway?" shouted Leon the Border Guard.

"As long as we stay out of the Short-Term Residency Zone, we don't have to pay the Tax," shouted someone from the pile. "Isn't that right?"

The Outer Hornerites looked at Phil, the recently appointed Special Border Activities Coordinator.

"Well of course that's right," said Phil. "Why would we charge you a tax for being in our country if you weren't even in our country, you morons?"

Just then the big pile of Inner Hornerites came tumbling down into Outer Horner.

This was unprecedented. Never before had so many Inner Hornerites infiltrated so deeply into Outer Horner. Leon frantically rang the loud buzzer that meant Invasion in Progress and the Outer Horner Militia (Freeda, Melvin, and Larry) quickly outflanked and surrounded the entire population of Inner Horner.

"This is an outrage!" Phil shouted. "Halt! Advance no farther! Invade us no more! Do you surrender? Surrender at once! Drop your weapons! Does everyone see how forceful

I'm being? As Special Border Activities Coordinator, I command you!"

The Inner Hornerites had no weapons, and no desire to invade Outer Horner, and were still dizzy from their fall, although a few of the less-dizzy Inner Hornerites were, in spite of themselves, sneaking dazed, curious glances over at the Outer Horner Cafe.

"We're not invading anybody," said Elmer. "We just tipped over."

"Return to the Short-Term Residency Zone at once!" shouted Phil. "With your hands up!"

So the Inner Hornerites raised their hands and stepped back over the green string into the Short-Term Residency Zone.

"Now that we have totally subdued you," Phil shouted, "allow me to remind you that you still owe us four smolokas."

"Well, we still don't have it," said Elmer. "You know very well we don't."

"Larry," shouted Phil. "Inventory their resources!"

Larry looked at Phil blankly.

"I thought we already took everything," Larry whispered.

"Look harder, Larry," said Phil. "Exhibit more vigilance."

Larry looked harder, exhibiting more vigilance.

"Well sir," he finally said. "The only thing I could find? Other than additional dirt? And I'm not sure this counts? Is that they're wearing clothes, on their bodies, sir."

"Well done, Larry," said Phil. "An excellent observation. Clothes are indeed a resource."

"Wait a minute," said Cal. "You're not proposing to take our clothes?"

"If you take our clothes, we'll be naked," said Wanda.

"But at least you'll have your taxes paid," said Phil, and gestured to Leon, who pushed his way into the Short-Term Residency Zone and started removing Old Gus's shirt.

"Hey, stop it!" shouted Old Gus. "My scar will show!"

"He's very sensitive about his scar," said Wanda.

But Leon kept tugging on Old Gus's shirt, and soon both nations could plainly see Old Gus's scar, and hear, from his Entwhistle Slit, the whirring noise that meant he was frustrated beyond speech and would any second now burst into tears while emitting clouds of green steam from his Leftmost Vent.

"Oh, that's enough," said Wanda, taking a swat at Leon's pointy hat.

"My God, Leon's under attack!" shouted Larry, and rushed into the Short-Term Residency Zone, causing Carol and Cal to inadvertently reinvade Outer Horner and Leon to bash his right Brow Clip into his own spadelike tail. Leon sprung from the hole, hatless and terrified, with a swollen bleeding Brow Clip, having failed to collect the taxes, and dove back into Outer Horner, while Phil heroically rescued Larry by pulling him out of the Short-Term

Residency Zone by his belt loops.

Both sides stood gasping on their respective sides of the green string, shocked at this sudden outburst of violence.

Phil stamped his foot, and his brain slid down his rack and rolled across the ground, and his central bladder inflated to the bursting point, and his Phalen Extender began slapping back and forth against his secondary spout.

"Your disgraceful attitude!" he bellowed in the stentorian voice, "being the result of centuries of taking our people for granted, habitually manifests itself in arrogance, an arrogance that has as its seed the apparent belief that we are less than you and must be subjugated. But we will not be subjugated! We are a noble people, of ancient lineage, and have a right to live and thrive, whereas you, who would take away our right to live and thrive, I'm not sure about you, I'm not sure that you have not, over the long years of taking advantage of our simple generous nature, forfeited certain rights having to do with your continued existence!"

Now, Larry knew Phil from high school, and knew that the longer Phil's brain stayed off, the less sense he would make, until finally his brain-rack would spasm and he would run totally out of juice. Once, Phil had run out of juice during a swim meet and sunk to the bottom of the pool, after which he had been winched out of the pool and connected to a Farley ReMotivator. For weeks afterward, the popular kids had mocked Phil mercilessly, even inventing a dance called The Phil, which involved making an awkward desperate jerky motion with one's torso, which, apparently, was what he had done while on the Farley ReMotivator.

"Phil, sir?" Larry said now, meekly. "May I remount your brain for you?"

"This is not about my brain!" shouted Phil. "It's these idiots who've got the brain problem. They owe us taxes! And have refused via violence to pay those taxes! In light of the heinous events of this outrageous day, which shall henceforth be known as Dark Dark Thursday, but also in light of the valor we Outer Hornerites have shown on this memorable and historic day, which will henceforth also be known as Amazing Heroic Thursday, I hereby declare a Federal Tax Mercifulness Occasion. An FTMO. Yes, an FTMO of celebration. That's it. And I declare this FTMO not out of fear, not at all, but out of pride, pride in our strength! Let us return to the capital on this joyous FTMO, to celebrate our astonishing victory!"

And Phil, carrying his brain under one arm, led his flustered Militia away from the border, hissing at them now and then to stop looking back so fearfully over their shoulders.

* * *

That evening Phil stormed around the disgusting southern portion of Outer Horner City in a frenzy. His brain had been knocked out of round by its recent smashing and sat crookedly in its rack, and now and then a spark flew out of his nosehole and his Phalen Extender flipped up for no apparent reason. Those stupid Inner Hornerites! How he hated them! Wasn't it just like them to sit like inert slugs on borrowed land, then suddenly erupt into inexplicable pointless violence! Here he was, finally starting to get a little something for himself, and they dared openly mock the authority of the President's Special Border Activities Coordinator, via bloodying Leon's Brow Clip? It was so frustrating! If only there was no Inner Horner, the Border Area would look so nice, and he could move on to more substantial Border Area issues, such as making the Border Area look even nicer. And he imagined the Border Area free of Inner Hornerites, enhanced by a Museum, a Museum of Outer Horner Culture, and in front of the Museum would stand a statue of him, Phil, and around the statue he imagined a group of swooning Outer Horner girls, with that classic Outer Horner beauty, and just as he was, in his mind, about to approach them and introduce himself as Phil, founder of the Museum and President of the nation, he turned a corner and almost ran into two enormous young men with rippling biceps and cruel beautiful faces, being methodically covered in mud by a tiny old woman on a ladder.

"Forget it, I'm not hiring," the old woman said. "I've got enough. I've got two. Two is plenty."

"I'm not looking for work," Phil said. "I'm the Special Border Activities Coordinator."

"Sure you are, sure you are," said the old woman. "And I'm the Queen of Mud."

"Why are you doing that?" said Phil.

"We're testing it out," she said. "To see if it's good. Look close. See how some of it's runny and some of it's nice and firm?"

"Why do you care?" Phil said.

"Why do we care!" she said. "You'd think you'd know that, if you're really the Special Activities Border Whatever Whatever. We care because we gotta write it on the package. Either 'Runny' or 'Nice, Firm.' That's why. Now move along. I'm not hiring."

"How much do you fellows get paid for this?" Phil asked the enormous muscular young men.

"Don't talk to them," the old woman said. "They're on the clock. They don't get paid nothing. They're apprentices. When they really learn how to do it, then they get paid."

"Not much of a job," said Phil.

"Well, sir, it's a living," said the first mud-covered young man.

"Anyways, it will be," said the second. "Someday. After our apprenticeships."

"And it sure beats being back home," said the first.

"Back home, when Ma covered us in mud or grease or lard?" said the second. "Not only did we not get paid, she'd yell at us while she did it."

"Edna never yells at us," said the first.

"Well, I like you boys," said Edna. "You boys have potential."

"Did you hear that, Vance?" said the first boy. "Edna said we have potential."

"Wow, I am so moved by that," said Vance. "Jimmy, can you imagine Ma ever saying something that nice to us?"

"The only nice thing Ma ever said to us?" said Jimmy. "Was once she said we looked slightly better in lard than in mud."

"Guys," said Phil. "You look pretty strong. Are you pretty strong?"

"Oh, we're strong," said Vance.

"Not to brag," said Jimmy, "but we really are strong. Watch this, sir."

And Jimmy lifted Edna between two fingers and set her on top of his head.

"All right, all right, mister comedian," said Edna. "Put me down. Back to work."

Jimmy put Edna down and she climbed back up her ladder and again started applying mud to his neck.

"Maybe you guys would like to come work for me," said Phil.

"What?" said Jimmy. "Wow, I can't believe it. On the very same day, Edna says we have potential and this guy tries to hire us!"

"Pretty big day, all right," said Vance.

"What exactly would we have to do, sir?" said Jimmy.

"Well," said Phil. "You'd be sort of like special friends of mine. Like bodyguards. You'd just do whatever I told you. Out at the Inner Horner border. I do a lot of work out at the Border, national security work."

"Bodyguards, wow!" said Jimmy. "National security work, wow! No offense, Edna, but I think bodyguard sounds even more impressive than Mud-Consistency Testing Associate."

"You boys aren't smart enough," said Edna.

"You're probably right," said Vance.

"Oh, they're smart enough," said Phil. "They're exactly the level of smart I'm looking for."

"Wow, Vance, did you hear that?" said Jimmy. "We're exactly the right level of smart!"

"Edna, we have to try it," said Vance. "Don't you see? This could be our big chance. Sir, how much would you pay?"

"Vance, God, don't be pushy," said Jimmy. "We don't necessarily have to get paid."

"A smoloka each," said Phil.

"Wow, that's pretty good," said Vance. "A whole

33

smoloka. I mean, if we could make it last, that could be really good. Jimmy, if we wanted to make that one smoloka last the rest of our lives, how much would we be allowed to spend each day?"

"Well, that depends on how long we're going to live," said Jimmy. "And we don't know that yet."

"He's better at math than me," explained Vance.

"I don't think you understand," said Phil. "That's a smoloka a day. One smoloka for every day you work. It's a salary."

"Holy cow!" said Vance. "A smoloka a day! For every day we work! A salary! So that would be like, seven smolokas a week, if we worked seven days a week, right? Are there still seven days in a week? Anyway, wow, we'd be rich. And all we have to do is do whatever you say?"

"That would be easy for us," said Jimmy. "Ask Edna. Edna, wouldn't you say we're really good at doing whatever someone says?"

"They're excellent," said Edna. "Very obedient. Whatever you tell them to do, they immediately do it."

"That's because if we didn't do exactly what Ma said, she made us sleep in the yard with the dogs," Vance said. "And we had pretty mean dogs. And a pretty yucky yard."

"Right at the edge of a cliff," said Jimmy.

"Lost a lot of dogs that way," said Vance.

"So anyways we got excellent at obeying," said Jimmy.

"Watch this," said Vance. "Watch how obedient. Sir, tell us to do something. Anything."

"Tear down that shack," said Phil.

"This one?" said Vance. "This one here with the cute little rose garden?"

And Vance and Jimmy tore down the shack with their bare hands, with amazing speed, revealing a family sitting in their pajamas at a crooked kitchen table.

"What in the world?" said the father.

"Don't even think about mouthing off to my brother, man!" shouted Vance.

"And don't even think about mouthing off to my brother, man!" shouted Jimmy, and lifted up the father by one leg, after which the father got very quiet.

"You're hired," said Phil.

"Ha!" said Jimmy, dropping the father back in the rubble that had been his shack. "What an amazing day."

"Hang on, Jimmy," said Vance. "I have an additional request. Before we sign on."

"Vance, jeez!" whispered Jimmy. "Don't get all demanding! You'll screw it up!"

"Jimmy, don't worry, I know what I'm doing," said Vance. "What I want, sir, to, uh, request, additionally? Is that, every now and then, you say something nice about us. If that's not too much. Like you could say something about how much potential we have, or how obedient we are, it doesn't even need to be true. Just something nice to us every day."

"We didn't get much of that at home," said Jimmy. "Mostly it was just, you know, Jimmy you jerk, how did you get so dumb? That sort of thing."

"Or like: Vance, you're pathetic, why did you even have to be born," said Vance.

"Or like: Jimmy, if I had to throw either you or one of the dogs off the cliff, I'd throw you," said Jimmy.

"I'll tell you what," said Phil. "Every day, in addition to your smoloka, I'll say something nice about each of you."

"About *each* of us?" said Vance. "Oh wow, I was just thinking you'd say something nice about one of us. Like one per day? Alternating? But now you're saying you'll say something nice about each of us every single day? Plus the smoloka?"

"A smoloka each," said Phil. "Do you understand that?"

"A smoloka *each*?" said Jimmy.

"Wow," said Vance. "Wow wow wow. I'm getting dizzy here."

"You dream and you dream," said Jimmy. "And one day it all comes true."

"Well, Edna," said Vance. "I guess this is goodbye."

"We've got to do it, Edna," said Jimmy. "Don't you see? Please don't be mad."

"Don't sweat it," said Edna. "You'll be easy to replace."

"I'm sure that's true," said Jimmy.

"We're certainly nothing special," said Vance.

"Let's get you fellows cleaned up," said Phil.

"You're going to *clean us up*?" said Jimmy.

"And get you some uniforms," said Phil.

"You're going to get us *uniforms*?" said Vance.

With tears of gratitude in their eyes, Jimmy and Vance followed Phil out of the disgusting part of town.

Next morning Phil and the Outer Horner Militia arrived at the border, accompanied by Vance and Jimmy, who were now wearing tight red t-shirts that read: "Phil's Special Friends."

"Tax time, tax time," said Phil. "And don't even think of grabbing Leon's hat. The way I figure it, you owe us four smolokas for Dark Dark Thursday and four for today, which I am hereby declaring the Memorable Friday of Total Triumphant Retribution. So eight smolokas. Leon, inventory their resources."

Leon, very cautiously, bandage on his Brow Clip, holding his hat on with both hands, walked around the Short-Term Residency Zone, squinting his eyes.

"Still just the clothes," he said.

"Kindly collect the taxes," Phil said to Jimmy and

Vance, who entered the Short-Term Residency Zone like twin grinning mountains, if twin grinning mountains could crack their knuckles while flexing their pecs and chomping gum, and soon shirts and pants and shoes and socks were flying over their tremendous shoulders into Outer Horner, where they were collected into a sack by Leon.

When Jimmy and Vance stepped away, there were the Inner Hornerites, totally naked.

"Freeda," said Phil. "Assess the value of these clothes. Is the total value of these clothes exactly eight smolokas?"

"I'm not sure," said Freeda, a little taken aback by the sight of so many naked blushing ashamed Inner Hornerites scrambling to stand behind one another.

"I think what you mean to say is yes, Freeda," said Phil sternly.

"Okay," said Freeda. "Yes."

"Super," said Phil. "Taxes paid. Enjoy the rest of your day, folks."

And Phil and the Special Friends and the Outer Horner Militia walked off, sorting through the clothes as they went.

"My God, those guys were strong," said Wanda.

"They were incredibly strong," said Curtis.

"This is terrible," said Elmer. "So humiliating."

"On the other hand, you know, nakedness is completely

natural," said Carol.

"That's true, I guess, Carol," said Cal. "I mean, our naked bodies are nothing to be ashamed of. Although guys? Actually? I'd prefer you guys didn't look at my wife."

"Also?" said Wanda. "Would you guys mind not looking at me? I feel so fat."

"Why are you all staring at my scar?" said Old Gus.

"Maybe we should just agree not to look at one another," said Wanda.

"Oh, this is crazy," Curtis said. "How long are we going to take this? We've got to *do* something. We've got to start resisting."

"Oh right, Curtis, let's resist," said Wanda. "Don't you get it? If we resist, they'll crush us. Did you see the size of those guys?"

"Cal, you're the one I don't get," said Curtis. "Here's your wife, naked and being displayed to the world, here's your shivering hungry kid, and what are you doing about it? Don't you love them? Don't you care?"

"Curtis, leave Cal alone," said Carol. "He's doing the best he can."

"Carol, please don't speak harshly to Curtis," said Wanda. "He was only expressing his opinion."

"Look at us bickering," said Curtis.

"I don't consider this bickering," said Wanda.

"Well, I do," said Curtis.

"It could be worse," said Elmer.

Everyone looked at Elmer.

"I thought we agreed not to look at one another," said Elmer, and for the rest of the day the Inner Hornerites stood staring straight ahead, except for Cal, who now and then snuck a guilty ashamed look over at Carol and Little Andy.

Then it was dusk, and the bright spotlight came on.

All night a bitter wind blew, causing icicles to form around the Inner Horner exhaust ports and steam vents, which made it even more galling when the Outer Horner Militia arrived at dawn wearing articles of former Inner Horner clothing over their Militia Uniforms.

"Good morning all," said Phil, wearing what appeared to be Wanda's former stocking cap on his brain. "What time is it, Leon?"

"Tax time, sir," said Leon.

"Bingo," said Phil.

The Inner Hornerites were silent.

"Look, what the heck am I supposed to do about this?" said Phil. "You people owe us four smolokas. There's a law, you know the law, yet you insist on defying the law. I am really at a loss here."

"Maybe they could run a tab?" said Freeda.

"Freeda, I appreciate your input," said Phil. "But do you really think these people are going to pay a tab? Are these trustworthy people? Honorable people? Did they or did they not recently attack Leon, leaving him bloody? Have you already forgotten the nightmare that was Dark Dark Thursday?"

"Maybe we could sell tickets?" said Melvin. "Sell tickets to people who want to, you know, sort of stare at them? Because they're naked and all?"

"Melvin, no," said Phil. "I mean, I like the idea conceptually, but the thing is, one, people can stare at them now, for free, so why impose additional costs on our people, and two, who the heck wants to stare at them anyway? They don't look so good. Except for Carol. Carol, I have to say, looks pretty good. Carol I would possibly pay to look at. Don't you guys think Carol looks pretty good?"

And Larry and Melvin and Leon and Phil's Special Friends all took a long look at Carol and agreed that she looked pretty good, good enough that they would possibly pay to look at her.

If someone had bothered to take a look at Cal, they would have noticed that his tuna fish can was trembling and his belt buckle was starting to glow.

"Look, here's an idea," said Phil. "I don't think it's any big secret that I've always had a thing for Carol. How about you people give me Carol, for my wife or whatever, and I give you, not just four smolokas, but *twelve* smolokas? That's enough for three days' taxes. What do you say? That sounds fair, doesn't it?"

At this Cal burst out of the Short-Term Residency Zone, blatantly invading Outer Horner, and threw himself at Phil so savagely, while angrily gnashing the lid of his tuna fish can, that Phil's gasket cover flew off and his brain came sliding off his rack and it took both Special Friends to finally pry Cal off of Phil's neck/sternum assembly.

"You little creep!" bellowed Phil. "You've damaged my gasket cover! How dare you attempt a revolution! The gasket cover of the Special Border Activities Coordinator!"

Jimmy was now holding Cal high up in the air, higher than Cal had ever been in his life, while Larry and Melvin scrambled to recover Phil's brain.

"You people," Phil shouted in the stentorian voice, "via shiftlessness and inertia, have forced us, a normally gentle constituency, into the position of extracting water from the recalcitrant stone of your stubbornness, by positing us as aggressors, when in fact we are selflessly lending you precious territory, which years ago was hewed by our ancestors from a hostile forbidding wilderness! When I think of my poor, dead grandparents, how hard they hewed, and here you come, sneaking into their sacred former wilderness to murder us in our beds via stealth! But shoulder that musket we must, that musket of subduing you, and this we will, using our usual indomitable methodology and excellent creativity and spirit of love. I don't dare undertake such a huge momentous decision on my own, since we are a democracy, so I suggest we take an urgent vote. Let us vote urgently: Do we or do we not enact my momentous decision?"

"But what is it?" said Melvin. "What is your momentous decision?"

"Do you really want to quarrel with your leader at a time like this, Melvin?" said Phil. "Is this really the time for naysaying? Do we or do we not enact my momentous decision, namely, to disassemble this aggressor? Freeda, please tally the vote."

"Disassemble him?" said Freeda. "Can we do that?"

"Guys!" shouted Cal from way up high, upside down. "Now's the time! It's now or never! Join me! Join the fight!"

"Listen to that little rat!" said Phil. "Still advocating violence!"

The other Inner Hornerites, seeing Jimmy's rippling biceps and cruel expression as he dangled Cal over the Cafe, imagined themselves suspended over the Cafe, about to be disassembled, and each decided, in his or her own way, that it was not, perhaps, at this time, entirely prudent to join the fight, and opted instead to stare down mutely at the green string, except for Carol, who stared up at Cal while blinking back tears and trying to restrain Little Andy, who was desperately trying to join the fight.

"May I please have a vote?" said Phil. "Do we or do we not disassemble this aggressor, for the good of the nation, in the interest of preventing further violence?"

And the citizens of Outer Horner, casting nervous sideways glances at one another, unanimously voted to support Phil in his decision to disassemble Cal, for the good of the nation, in the interest of preventing further violence.

"Kindly enact the will of the nation!" Phil said to the Special Friends.

The Special Friends leaned down over Cal and, using a socket set and a pair of pliers, enacted the will of the nation.

Soon Cal was reduced to a limp belt buckle and a tuna fish can and the blue dot and a few connecting parts.

"I guess we were wrong when we thought they had no additional assets," Phil said. "Actually they've got plenty of additional assets. A nation's most important asset is its people, don't you think? Freeda, how much would you say this bundle of additional assets is worth? This pile of junk? Four smolokas? Would you say the tuna fish can is worth two and the belt buckle is worth one and the blue dot and various connecting parts are worth a total of one?"

"Okay," said Freeda, trying to keep from crying.

"Congratulations," said Phil to the Inner Hornerites.

"Taxes paid. Thanks so much."

Then Phil reracked his brain and directed Leon to in-carcerate the various parts of Cal at several discrete loca-tions across the length and breadth of Outer Horner, in the interest of national security.

Leon, using a wheelbarrow, incarcerated Cal's tuna fish can in Far South Distant Outer Horner, a region dotted with thousands of tiny identical lakes, and incarcerated Cal's belt buckle in Far East Distant Outer Horner, a lush verdant zone where cows' heads grew out of the earth shouting sarcastic things at anyone who passed, which, though lush and verdant, was unpopulated because the cows' sarcasm was so withering, and incarcerated Cal's var-ious connecting parts in Far West Distant Outer Horner, where pairs of trees made X shapes as far as the eye could see.

This left only Cal's blue dot, which, per Phil, was placed in a glass case a few hundred feet from Inner Horner, as a warning and a reminder to the other Inner Hornerites, who all night long, from the Short-Term Residency Zone, watched the sad blue dot that had formerly been Cal's torso expand and contract, as if hyperventilating, or sobbing.

* * *

Freeda of the Outer Horner Militia had always felt that she'd been built too wide at the bottom and thin at the top, and because of her shape and her extensive shoulder and torso foliage had, several times, when pausing in public, been mistaken for a shrub or small tree and, in fact, the Christmas she was eight, having paused to gaze up in wonder at the stars, had come home in tears, covered with lights and glass balls. So it was a great delight to her when her only child, Gertrude, grew into a tall beautiful preteen with no foliage at all, who took dance lessons and could gaze at the stars for hours without ever once coming home decorated.

That night Freeda had a dream. In her dream, Gertrude was a tall beautiful vase belonging to Phil, who kept holding Gertrude up to the light, looking for flaws. Freeda was a small furry dog, who kept leaping up, trying to bite Phil as he inspected Gertrude.

"Put her down, put her down," Freeda barked at him. "Why do you want to be so bad?"

"I am not bad," said Phil. "I am totally good. What I do, benefits all."

Then Phil found a flaw and threw Gertrude against the wall, breaking her into a thousand pieces.

Freeda woke and rushed to Gertrude's room. Relieved to find that Gertrude was not a broken vase and that her pink shelving was still intact, she gave Gertrude a kiss on the middle of her three rosy cheeks.

"Snowing on my face," Gertrude mumbled.

Then Freeda went to her desk and wrote a note to the President.

Dear Mr. President, it read. *Today Phil, whom I previously so much respected, disassembled a fellow, an Inner Horner fellow, who seemed nice enough, and even had a family. Is this what we stand for here in Outer Horner? I hope not. Our country is big, let us be big. Phil is out of control, sir, and must be stopped. Please do something. We're all counting on you.*

Then she put on a cloak with a hood, walked to the Presidential Palace, and slid her note under the huge jeweled door.

The lowliest butler read the note and passed it to a slightly less lowly butler, who passed it to the mirror-faced Advisor, who read it with grave concern and passed it on to the President.

"This is an outrage!" shouted the President. "Isn't it? Isn't it an outrage?"

"That depends, sir," said the Advisor. "Do you think it is?"

"Well, it seems to me it is," said the President. "Although I could be wrong. But we've never done that before, have we, this disassembling business?"

"Not unless you say we have," said the Advisor.

"Get me Phil!" thundered the President.

"But sir," said the Advisor, "I'm not sure, in light of your condition—"

"What condition?" thundered the President. "I don't have any condition. Are you saying I have a condition? Are you saying I'm somehow getting worse or something? Are you saying I'm so old and fat and nostalgic that I'm becoming increasingly ineffectual and am always repeating myself in a state of perpetual confusion?"

"No sir," said the mirror-faced Advisor. "I'm not saying that at all. You are no more old or fat or nostalgic or ineffectual than you were yesterday."

"Really?" said the President. "Do you really think so? Thanks. Thanks for saying that. Look, let's get this Phil fellow in here and clear this thing up before I forget how I feel about it and/or misplace this note."

So the mirror-faced Advisor passed a note to the squat greenish skulky guy in charge of delivering messages, who went skittering over to Phil's crummy apartment and slipped it under Phil's nicked-up door.

What's all this about disassembling someone? the note read. *The President will see you first thing tomorrow morning.*

* * *

The Presidential Palace was a gleaming gold-domed build-
ing with a vast high-ceilinged Entry Hall, decorated with
paintings of various types of animals the President liked to
eat, served on plates, although in the paintings the animals
were still alive and had all their fur on and looked a little
panicked.

As Phil entered the Intermediate Hall with the Special
Friends, the mirror-faced Advisor pulled him aside.

"First of all, let me say," whispered the Advisor, "in
terms of the President's condition, that I don't want to im-
ply that there are problems, with the President, with the
President's health, especially with his mental health, in
terms of how nostalgic and ineffectual he's become."

"What Al is trying to say?" said a second Advisor, who
had three identical smiles, one beneath the other on his
perfectly round face. "Is that he is not, by pulling you aside
like this and denying that the President is growing ever
more batty, implying in any way that the President is in
fact growing ever more batty."

"Absolutely," said the mirror-faced Advisor. "That is exactly what I am not saying. And furthermore, I am also not
saying that we should work together to ensure that the entirely false news of the President's alleged recent battiness
not travel beyond these walls. On the contrary, I encourage
you to think and say whatever you like, once you leave here,
bearing in mind, please, that a weak, infirm, half-crazed

President would not at all be the worst thing that could happen to a country that finds itself threatened by a hostile bordering power."

"If we had that sort of President," said the very smiley Advisor.

"Which we don't," said the mirror-faced Advisor.

"Unless you notice that we do," said the very smiley Advisor.

"In which case we might," said the mirror-faced Advisor.

"We could discuss that," said the very smiley Advisor.

"The President will see you now!" boomed a third Advisor, basically just a mouth wearing a wig.

Phil entered the Great Hall. The President, surrounded by tables of souvenirs from his illustrious career, looked even fatter than he had looked at the border and seemed to have sprouted several additional mustaches.

"Phil!" said the President. "So nice to see you! Isn't that your name? Oh, I remember that time at the border. What a sweet time that was! We won't see the likes of those days again, will we? Sit down, dear boy. How do I look? I bet I look fatter than ever. Plus sadder. Lately I'm so sad. Do you know what I was thinking about? Just now? I was just now thinking about that wonderful time when you walked in just now! Remember that? I was so happy to see you! I remember that time so well! We won't see the likes of those days again, will we? And you know what else I remember fondly? The time, just now, after you walked in, when I asked you to sit down, dear boy. Do you remember that? How I sort of patted the seat, the seat you are now sitting on? Oh, sweet memories! Wasn't that a time! We won't see the likes of those days again, will we? Everything passes so quickly in this life! It seems like just yesterday I was young and powerful, and now look at me, I can't even get up. Too fat, I guess. Whereas even this morning, I could get up. Remember that, Al, remember this morning when I stood right up? We won't see the likes of those days again, will we? I hopped right up, didn't I?"

"Yes you did," said the mirror-faced Advisor, giving Phil a look.

"I've been working very hard today, Phil," the President said. "What I've mainly been working on is, first, trying to remember why I called you here, and second, deciding what to feel weepy about. Because lately my weeping has become a little unfocused. In the middle of weeping about my weight, I find myself suddenly weeping about my legacy. In the middle of weeping about something I should've said fifty years ago, I suddenly find myself weeping about the rate at which my pants seem to be getting tighter. And then suddenly I pause in my weeping to sit for hours at a time, re-creating my childhood home in my mind. Nothing gets done! It's become clear that I need a weeping schedule. That way, you know, you look at your watch, you look at your schedule, you know what you're weeping about. Phil, do you remember why I called you here?"

"Yes, Mr. President," said Phil. "You called me here for a report on the situation at the border. And I'm happy to report that I was recently able to gracefully quell a disturbing outbreak of violence at the border by enacting certain physical rearrangements designed to prevent further outbreaks of violence, thus rendering the instigator of the violence incapable of instigating further violence, via separating the instigator's component parts and relocating them in discrete physical locations."

"Curt," said the President, to the Advisor who was a mouth wearing a wig. "Do you remember that time, I don't know when it was, when you came in here and said I had a visitor? And I said, Curt, show him in? Oh, those were the days. When was that? Who was that?"

"That was just now, sir," said Curt. "I said that when Phil here arrived."

"We won't see the likes of those days again, will we?" said the President. "Al, would you mind weighing me again? I'm curious. Also, let's count these mustaches again. I feel like I've sprouted a few, even since those halcyon days way back when, this morning, when I hopped right up."

So the mirror-faced Advisor lifted the President onto a

scale while the smiley Advisor counted the President's mustaches and confirmed that the President now had eighteen mustaches, whereas this morning he'd only had sixteen.

"Oh, this morning," said the President. "Blessed time of sixteen mustaches and hopping right up. What did you want to see me about, Phil? Or did I want to see you? Did I summon you?"

Phil had a sick feeling but also an excited feeling. This was his President? This man was running his beloved Outer Horner? If Inner Horner mounted a full-scale invasion, this was the man who'd be leading the fight? He'd had the vague sense, out at the Border, that the President was not quite as sharp, perhaps, as himself, Phil, but now it was suddenly obvious that he, Phil, was his floundering nation's only hope.

"Phil," said the President, looking up at the Special Friends. "Who are these lads? Makes me remember my youth, when I was big and muscular. Are they strong? They certainly are big enough."

"They are very strong," said Phil. "May I demonstrate?"

"Please," said the President.

"Jimmy," said Phil. "Lift off the dome."

And Jimmy stood up straight and lifted the Palace dome over his head with one hand.

"Ha ha!" said the President. "Bravo! Look at those birds flying in! That's really something."

"Now, Jimmy," said Phil. "Step over that wall, while still holding the dome, and take the dome over to my apartment. Then come right back."

"This I've got to see!" said the President, clapping his hands with delight.

And Jimmy stepped over the wall of the Palace, still holding the dome, and disappeared in the direction of Phil's apartment.

"Well, we certainly get a lot more sun this way, don't we?" said the President. "How about that other one? Is he strong too?"

"Vance," said Phil. "Take a wall under each arm. And carry them to my apartment."

"Ha!" said the President. "That will be hard. A wall under each arm. Ha! Did you hear that, Ed?"

"Yes sir, I did," said the smiley Advisor, looking at Phil with new respect.

Vance placed the north wall of the Palace under one arm and the south wall under the other, stepped over the east wall, and disappeared in the direction of Phil's apartment.

"Oh boy!" said the President. "All we've got left is two walls! I have to admit, I'm feeling sort of nostalgic for the time when I had not only four walls, but a roof. I could just weep! Remember that, Al, when we had all our walls? However, I'm also looking forward to the time when my ceiling and walls are brought back, which I'm sure will be soon. Won't it? Won't it be soon?"

Jimmy returned, domeless, and stepped over the east wall.

"Now watch this, Mr. President," said Phil. "You might think Jimmy here would be a little tired, but no. Watch this. Jimmy, take the other two walls, one under each arm, and sprint to my apartment."

"Sprint?" said the President. "Are you sure he's not overdoing it? We wouldn't want him to strain himself."

Jimmy tucked the east wall under one arm and the west wall under the other, and took off at a sprint in the direction of Phil's apartment.

"Well, well," said the President. "I congratulate you! Those are two very strong boys. And they work for you? My Advisors, I like them well enough, but I don't think they could do that. Do you boys think you could do that?"

The Advisors mumbled that, no, they probably couldn't exactly do that.

"Well, Mr. President," said Phil. "I'd best be going. I have to get back to the border and collect my taxes."

"Ha ha!" said the President. "You, Phil, are a real go-getter. I admire that. Just, you know, have those large boys return my Palace whenever it's convenient. When do you think it will be? In an hour or so? Sometime later today?"

"I'm pretty busy today," said Phil. "I have problems at the border, as I've said."

"Tomorrow then?" said the President.

"Tomorrow's also not good," said Phil.

"Well, Phil," said the President. "As President I, you know, sort of need my Palace, otherwise . . ."

"Actually I think I'm going to keep the Palace awhile," said Phil.

"Well, Phil," said the President. "I don't know how I feel about that. You're not the President, I'm the President, I'm the one wearing the Presidential Cravat, and so, it would seem to me that I would be the one to decide when you should bring my Palace back. Right? Am I right in that, Al?"

The mirror-faced Advisor said nothing.

"That's a nice cravat," said Phil.

"Yes, yes it is," said the President. "Would you like to see it? If I let you see it, will you think about returning my Palace?"

"I'd love to see it," said Phil, and took the Presidential Cravat off the President and put it on himself.

"Well, it looks nice on you," said the President.

"Looks very nice on him," said the mirror-faced Advisor.

"Super on him," said the very smiley Advisor.

"Oh, I remember the time when I used to wear that

Presidential Cravat," mumbled the President. "It seems like ages ago. But it was just minutes ago, wasn't it?"

"Yes it was," said Phil.

There among the President's many mustaches bloomed a slow look of understanding.

"We won't see the likes of those days again, will we?" said the President.

"No we won't," said Phil.

"Mr. President?" said the mirror-faced Advisor. "Mr. Former President? May I just say what a pleasure it's been serving you, even in this time of twilight and diminishing strength. Although I would be remiss, sir, if I didn't add that I feel it was somewhat injurious for me, in the prime of my career, to have been serving you, someone growing increasingly weak, when I could've been serving someone strong and getting stronger. Strength is, sir, and I expect always will be, a lure for the ambitious and clever. Phil here has, sir, I think you must admit, a great deal of strength. He is not only strong, but getting stronger, I think you must agree, and—"

"Are you leaving me, Al?" said the President.

"I'm afraid so," said the mirror-faced Advisor.

"And are you leaving me, Ed?" said the President to the smiley Advisor. "Leaving me for Phil? Are you all leaving me? Is Phil now the President? Is that what you boys are saying?"

The smiley Advisor lowered his eyes and one of his smiles turned sad.

"Oh," said the President. "How well I remember those distant times just this morning, when you all so reverently dressed me. I will never forget those times. I thank you for them. And Al? I'm not so sure about this Phil fellow. Careful, Al. This Phil, he's a little frightening. He gets things done, yes, but—"

"Excuse me, sir," said the mirror-faced Advisor. "I would ask you not to insult our President."

"That could be construed as treasonous," said the smiley Advisor.

"Ah," said the former President. "I see."

Then President Phil and his Advisors briskly left the former site of the Presidential Palace, which was now just a patch of extravagant flooring in the middle of a vast garden.

"Where to, Mr. President?" said the mirror-faced Advisor.

"To the Presidential Palace, of course," said Phil. "For my Inauguration, and my Inaugural Party."

"How wonderful!" said the mirror-faced Advisor. "A President who loves a good party."

"That former President?" said the smiley Advisor. "Never threw parties."

"Never once," said the mirror-faced Advisor, who had,

at one of the former President's frequent parties, gone overboard on glass cleaner and temporarily blinded himself, then bashed into the smiley-faced Advisor, sustaining a hairline crack between his eyes, about which he was still self-conscious.

"To the Presidential Palace!" shouted the Advisor who was just a mouth and a wig, throwing back his head so energetically that his wig flew off, and he therefore briefly became just a mouth.

At the new Presidential Palace, which was just the walls of the former Presidential Palace propped against Phil's apartment and crookedly capped with the golden dome, the Inaugural Party ran late into the night. The Outer Hornerites, deeply proud to be Outer Hornerites, staggered from wall to wall, overfilling their toluene receptacles and bellowing their national drinking song, "Large, Large, Large, Beloved Land (If Not the Best, Why So Very Dominant?)."

The Special Friends sat in a corner, wearing headphones, listening to personalized Tapes of Praise, made for them by Phil.

"Oh jeez," said Jimmy, too loudly. "He just said I have great biceps!"

"He just said, about me?" said Vance, also too loudly.

"That he loves the focused look I get on my face when following an order."

"He likes the way my lats flare when I pick someone up!" shouted Jimmy.

"I work well with others!" shouted Vance.

"There's a deep intelligence in me that others rarely see!" shouted Jimmy.

At the wild peak of the night, Phil mounted Jimmy's shoulders and, raising his Phalen Extender in a spastic victory salute, knocked off his own brain, which dropped into a bowl of chips.

"My people!" he shouted in the stentorian voice. "I shall speak now of us! Who are we? We are an articulate people, yet a people of few words. We feel deeply, yet refrain from embarrassing displays of emotion. Though firm, we are never too firm, though we love fun, we never have fun in a silly way that makes us appear ridiculous, unless that is our intent. Our national coloration, though varied, is consistent. Everything about us is as it should be, for example, we can be excessive, when excess is called for, and yet, even in our excess, we show good taste, although never is our taste so super-refined as to seem precious. Even the extent to which we are moderate is moderate, except when we have decided to be immoderately moderate, or even shockingly flamboyant, at which time our flamboyance is truly breathtaking in a really startling way, and when we decide to make mistakes, our mistakes are as big and grand and irrevocable as any nation's colossal errors, and when we decide to deny our mistakes, we sound just as if we were telling the truth, and when we decide to admit our errors, we do so in a way that is truly moving in its extreme frankness! Am I making sense? Am I saying this well?"

"Yes you are!" said Larry. "You're saying it very well!"

"Yes I am!" said Phil. "My saying it so well proves what I have just been saying, namely, that our ancient noble stock has, over many centuries of right living, evolved into the highest and most advanced nation there is, a nation that has, after many years of misrule by that chubby old guy, finally gotten the leader it deserves! That chubby old guy, in addition to being criminally forgetful, was recklessly flagrant. Knowing these Inner Hornerites were prone to unmotivated spasms of violence, he daily proclaimed, via that pathetic mere string of a border: Come in, invade us, feel free to commit your unmotivated violence spasms all over our sleeping innocent babies, while I obsess about my bellies and mustaches. Well, I am not flagrant or forgetful, I have one belly and no mustache, and my only obsession is the safety of my people, which is why I hereby proclaim, as my first Presidential Act, my innovative Border Area Improvement Initiative! Who is on board? Who will sign this Certificate of Total Approval, sanctioning my Initiative?"

"What does it say, sir?" said Melvin.

"Why do you care what it says, Melvin?" said Larry. "Don't you trust Phil?"

"Of course I trust Phil," said Melvin. "I trust Phil like twice as much as you trust Phil."

"Then why are you resisting signing the Certificate of Total Approval?" said Larry.

"Give me that thing, I'll sign it," said Melvin. "I'll sign it right now, without even reading it."

"I'll sign it without even looking at it," said Larry.

"I'll sign it with my eyes closed," said Leon the Border Guard.

"I'll sign it with my eyes closed, facing away from it," said Melvin.

So Larry and Melvin and Leon and the Special Friends and the Advisors lined up facing backwards, eyes closed, and signed the Certificate of Total Approval.

Even Freeda signed it, because everybody was staring at her.

"Excellent, Freeda, thanks so much!" said Phil. "All have signed. All Totally Approve of my Border Area Improvement Initiative. Although Freeda? Too bad you didn't sign it with your eyes closed while facing away from it. Not that I mind! You signed it, which is what matters, basically, I guess."

Just then from out in the street someone cleared his

throat so loudly that the bowl of chips bearing Phil's brain fell off the table, causing Phil's brain to roll under the couch.

"BUG CARRIES BREAD CRUMB!" shouted someone from outside. "OTHER BUGS LOOK ON IN AWED SILENCE!"

"WATER RUNS DOWNHILL TOWARDS SEWER!" shouted a second voice.

"AIR CONTINUES TO FLOAT AROUND, BEING BREATHED BY MANY!" shouted a third.

Looking out, Phil saw three handsome well-groomed squat little men with detachable megaphones growing out of their clavicles.

"MAN REGARDS STRANGERS IN STREET!" shouted the first little man.

"What are you guys doing?" asked Phil.

"MAN ASKS QUESTION, EXPECTS ANSWER!" said the third little man.

"MAJOR MEDIA FIGURES PREPARE TO RE-SPOND!" said the first man.

"IS THE MEDIA HELD TOO MUCH ACCOUNT-ABLE?" said the second.

"We're with the media," said the first man, in a normal tone of voice that issued not from the megaphone but from a toothy smile near his rear end.

"Not much happening out here," said the second man.

"So we're just practicing."

"In case someday something does happen," said the third little man.

"SKY REMAINS DARK AS NIGHT PROCEEDS!" said the first little man.

"Good one," said the second.

"I felt that was an important issue," said the first.

"MAJOR MEDIA FIGURE COMPLIMENTED BY SECOND MAJOR MEDIA FIGURE!" said the second little man.

"MAJOR MEDIA FIGURE ANNOUNCES COMPLIMENTING OF MAJOR MEDIA FIGURE BY SECOND MEDIA FIGURE!" shouted the third little man.

"IS THE MEDIA TOO FOCUSED ON THE MEDIA?" shouted the second little man.

"DOG PEES ON SHRUB, LOOKS ASKANCE AT OWN REAR!" shouted the first little man.

"You should come out to the Border Area tomorrow," Phil said. "Big things happening out there. We're dealing with a violent, irrational people who really hate us. The nation just Totally Approved my Border Area Improvement Initiative. So tomorrow we Implement. It won't be easy. Lots of heavy lifting. We've already accomplished a number of painful, difficult security-related tasks, but tomorrow we'll be attempting the most painful, difficult task of all. It would be super to have some skillful truth-tellers out there, encouraging the nation in its critical hour of destiny. I'd be happy to pay your expenses and a small stipend."

"Wait a minute," said the first little man. "Is that the Presidential Cravat you're wearing?"

"Oh my God," said the second little man. "Are you the President?"

"I thought the President was that little fat guy with the mustaches," said the third little man.

"That was the old President," said Phil.

The little media men were amazed and gratified that this new President possessed such a nuanced understanding of the vital role of the media, unlike the old President, who used to claim that their attempts to keep the nation informed made his bursitis worse and shattered the Presidential Cups in the Presidential Cupboard.

"NEW PRESIDENT VOWS TO ELIMINATE BORDER THREAT!" shouted the first little man.

"NEW PREZ TO NATION: YOU SHALL KNOW PEACE!" shouted the second.

"WHAT TIME SHOULD WE BE THERE?" shouted the third, who then realized he was presenting his personal views as the objective view of the media and asked his question more ethically, by asking it out the mouth near his rear.

"Things tend to start around dawn," said Phil.

"Then we'd better get practicing," said the third.

"MOON, STARS CONTINUE TO BE LOCATED IN SKY!" shouted the first little man.

"NEIGHBOR LADY DRAWS BLINDS WITH CRABBY LOOK ON FACE!" shouted the second.

"EXCLUSIVE SERIES ON BORDER AREA STRUGGLE STARTS TOMORROW!" shouted the third.

"I like the sound of that," said the first.

"I hope it's not too late to find flak jackets," said the second.

"Just save your receipts," said Phil.

The little men's voices drifted out across the farthest reaches of Outer Horner, until finally, because Outer Horner was not infinite, their voices drifted into the surrounding country of Greater Keller, which ran like a six-inch-wide circular strip of ribbon around Outer Horner.

Because Greater Keller was so thin it was almost nonexistent, it was rarely visited much less invaded, and was therefore very prosperous. The nine Greater Kellerites spent their days walking behind their President single-file, carefully placing one foot in front of the other, happy and cordial, engaged in endless energetic conversation about the appearance of the portion of Outer Horner they happened to be walking around, the nuances of the cup of coffee they were currently enjoying, and/or the enjoyable impression being made on them by the way the person in front of them looked when viewed from behind.

"Temporary Halt, please!" called President Rick, leaning into Outer Horner airspace, hand to his ear. "Someone is saying some rather loud and interesting things from Outer Horner, concerning a new President."

"I find myself wondering what happened to their old President," said the First Lady.

"Excellent point, dear!" said President Rick. "Let's discuss that. Let's have some good national conversation about that, thus increasing our National Enjoyment Level. Did he retire, one wonders? Was he forced out of office?"

"Did he pass away?" said the First Lady. "If so, were his last words inspirational?"

"Or was he perhaps bitter at the end?" said the First Daughter.

"Oh, I doubt it, dear," said the First Lady. "Remember when he visited?"

"What a sport!" said President Rick. "Such a fat little man, but did he ever give walking in a circle a good try!"

And the nation fondly remembered the former President of Outer Horner, one of its rare visitors who, finding it difficult to walk in a circle, given his three legs and multiple bellies, kept falling out of their nation and inadvertently returning to his own.

"Just who is this new President?" said Lenore, Citizen #5, meaning she was fifth in line. "Is he as good a sport as the old President? Does he like to talk? Is he sociable?"

"Can he walk in a circle?" said President Rick. "That's the main thing. Does he like to make pleasant conversation as he walks in a circle drinking coffee?"

"Does he even like coffee?" said Kevin, Citizen #8.

"Is he, perhaps, more of a tea drinker?" said the First Daughter.

The nation of Greater Keller went momentarily silent at this troubling thought.

"I think we should invite him for a Visit," said the First Lady. "For days before his Visit, we could look forward to his Visit. For days after his Visit, we could discuss how well his Visit went. Think how Enjoyable we'll find that!"

"Cliff?" said the President to Citizen #4. "How are we doing? How good, rich, and beautiful is our life at the moment? How fully are we living?"

"Well, sir," said Cliff, the National Enjoyment Assessor. "Our cups are approximately half-full, our coffee is still warm, the First Lady has just passed around some nice cookies, we've got the sudden surge of interest associated with the possible Visit of the President of Outer Horner—I'd say we're Enjoying at about an Eight of a possible Ten."

"Not bad," said President Rick. "We are really Enjoy-ing!"

"Life for us is rich," said the First Daughter.

Suddenly Kelli, Citizen #7, blew a whistle.

"Mid-Morning Reversal!" President Rick called hap-pily, and the population of Greater Keller lay flat on the ground so the President could take his rightful place at the front of the line, by stepping very gingerly over the prone forms of his people, after which the First Lady stepped gingerly over the prone population, after which the First Daughter and those behind her in line stepped gingerly over the prone population, until finally the Pres-ident stood at the head of a line that was now a mirror-image of its former self.

"Who would like to deliver our invitation?" said the President. "Dale? Would you mind?"

"It would be an honor, sir," said Dale, and the First Daughter blushed, because, unbeknownst to her parents, she was in love with Dale, who, unfortunately for her, was Citizen #9, which meant there were five citizens between her and Dale, and therefore they never got any time alone, except briefly during Reversals, when he was lying prone and she was stepping gingerly over him.

Dale shot a quick loving glance at the First Daughter, then advanced into Far West Distant Outer Horner via a series of large arcs, which was the only way Greater

Kellerites could walk, trained as they were from youth to circular motion.

If this mission was successful, Dale felt, it would put him in an excellent position to approach the President with a Line Position Change Request.

"Shall we?" said President Rick, and Kelli, Citizen #7, blew her whistle, and the Counter-Clockwise Morning Circumambulation began.

All morning and most of the afternoon the Inner Hornerites stood shivering in the Short-Term Residency Zone, waiting for Phil to arrive, deeply ashamed about what had happened to Cal. Like anyone deeply ashamed, they looked for someone to blame, and decided to blame Cal, who they all missed tremendously.

"What was that crazy guy thinking?" said Wanda. "I mean, jeez, what a hothead."

"When I advocated resistance I certainly didn't mean that," said Curtis, looking guiltily over at the little blue dot.

"What did you mean?" said Carol.

"Well, I meant some, ah, conversational resistance," Curtis said, blinking nervously. "A period during which we would say challenging but polite things, things which might cause them to possibly consider reassessing their positions vis-à-vis us."

Just then the Inner Hornerites heard a fanfare similar to the Presidential Fanfare, and saw what appeared to be the Presidential Board, being carried by what looked like a group of Presidential Advisors, except that, sitting where the President usually sat, sat someone who resembled Phil, had Phil been wearing a smug euphoric expression and the Presidential Cravat.

"You've got to be kidding," said Elmer.

Then Phil did something he had never done before: He yanked his own bolt. He yanked his bolt, feeling that, although he was feeling quite Presidential, he would feel even more Presidential once he got the rush of confidence he always felt when his brain slid off.

But when he yanked his bolt, nothing slid off.

His hands flew up to his rack and a sudden look of panic shot across his face.

With a sense of dread he remembered his spasming rack, the slow descent to the bottom of the high-school pool, waking up senseless on the Farley ReMotivator unable to make words, his arms and legs flailing, hydraulic oil running out of his Pan and into the floor drain.

"Boys!" he shouted frantically in the stentorian voice. "Quickly now! Implement Phase I!"

From a huge backpack the Special Friends took a posthole digger and eight stout posts and a roll of barbed wire, then dug eight quick holes around the perimeter of the Short-Term Residency Zone, dropped the posts in, nailed the barbed wire to the posts, and hung a sign reading: "Peace-Encouraging Enclosure."

"What, we're in jail?" said Elmer.

"You're putting us in jail now?" said Wanda.

"How typical of the Inner Horner mindset!" said Phil. "To be unable to distinguish a jail from a Peace-Encouraging Enclosure. Safe inside the Peace-Encouraging Enclosure, you will be protected from your innate violent tendencies, and we will be protected from you. It is a real win/win."

Just then the little media men came racing up, equipped with flak jackets and new megaphones twice the size of their former megaphones.

"Sorry we're late!" the first little man said from the mouth near his rear.

"What'd we miss?" said the second little man. "What's going on?"

"Phase I of the Border Area Improvement Initiative is complete," Phil said. "And we are rapidly moving on to Phase II."

The Special Friends disappeared behind the Outer Horner Cafe, and reemerged pushing an enormous wooden cart overflowing with soil, shovels, an apple tree, barrels of water, and what looked like an aquarium.

"Fill in that hole, boys!" Phil shouted. "Then plant the tree. And restore the stream. Make it wider than before. Also, stock it with fish! At last we are reclaiming our ancient ancestral land, and we want it to look nice!"

The Special Friends took off their shirts and put on tanning oil and in no time at all had filled in the former nation of Inner Horner, planted a new apple tree, dug a wider stream, and stocked the stream with fish.

"PREZ TRANSFORMS VIOLENT MUDDY HOLE INTO PASTORAL PARADISE!" shouted the first little man.

"PEACE FINALLY ACHIEVED AT PROBLEMATIC BORDER AREA!" shouted the second.

"VISIONARY LEADER DAZZLES NATION WITH DECISIVE GREATNESS!" shouted the third.

It was true, Phil realized. He was great. He had come so far from his humble beginnings. He remembered his pathetic childhood home, the family crammed into the little kitchen, his father sitting in the sink so his mother could open the refrigerator, his mother climbing on top of the refrigerator so his father could let down the ironing board. Then he remembered the dark days after his father left, when suddenly there was more room to get the refrigerator open but no reason to open it, since there was never anything inside. Why had Dad left? Phil knew very well why. One day they'd gone on a family picnic, to the Border Area, and Dad had been playfully throwing some rocks, small rocks, pebbles really, into Inner Horner, just for fun, when one of the Inner Hornerites, apparently unable to grasp the difficult concept of lighthearted playful joshing, claimed one of the pebbles had entered his Exhaust Port, and alerted the Border Guard, at that time a guy named Smitty, a humorless jerk with pronounced Inner Horner tendencies, who'd asked Dad to stop, since, strictly speaking, harassing Inner Hornerites was illegal. The look on poor Dad's face! He'd been so embarrassed. Phil felt certain that the humiliation of being publicly corrected in front of a bunch of smirking Inner Hornerites while his wife and child looked on had pushed Dad over the edge.

A week later Dad left, and Phil never saw him again.

Oh, if Dad could see him now! Dad had always said Inner Hornerites were the dirt of the world, and now the world was about to be cleansed of dirt, once and for all, by him, by Phil!

It was time for Phase III.

"My people!" he shouted in the stentorian voice. "As long as they are existent, they seem to keep rising up against us! Therefore, for us to be at total peace, they must be totally gone! Gone gone gone! Let us now create permanent peace, while simultaneously demonstrating good fiscal sense, by collecting the taxes in advance for the next five days, via collecting all their national assets at once, right now!"

"All of them?" said Freeda.

"The whole country?" said Melvin.

"Are we not us?" bellowed Phil. "Are they not them? Us being us, do we not, being fully good, have the right to end what, totally bad, threatens us, even in the slightest? Would it not be negligent to do otherwise?"

"Ah, here we go," muttered Old Gus, who was by now so hungry that whenever he tried to breathe he looked like he was smirking.

"What was that?" said Phil. "What are you smirking about?"

"I'm not smirking," said Gus. "I'm trying to breathe."

"Very funny!" thundered Phil, so loudly that Gus's left antler popped out.

Freeda stood frozen. Gertrude Gertrude Gertrude, she was thinking, what would Gertrude think if Gertrude learned her mother had once stood silently by while a trembling grandpa was disassembled? Freeda had nothing against this trembling grandpa, who actually looked very much like her own trembling grandpa, except her grandpa looked more like a *J* than a *C* and had branches, not antlers.

"Phil," Freeda said hoarsely, several leaves dropping off due to sudden dryness. "I'm not sure about this."

"You're not *sure* about this?" said Phil. "Freeda? Did you sign your Certificate of Total Approval? I believe you did. Although, as I recall, you signed it rather disrespectfully, with your eyes open, while facing it. That should have been my first clue that your Loyalty was suspect. Did you even read your Certificate of Total Approval before signing it, Freeda? Especially Paragraph D, Disloyalty Consequences? 'When Disloyalty occurs (to be determined at the discretion of PHIL), the consequence for that Disloyalty will be determined by PHIL and PHIL alone.' Therefore, since I simply can't have someone Disloyal around me, contaminating my nation, per my determination, will you hereby make things easier on yourself, by kneeling before the Special Friends with your primary connecting parts easily accessible?"

"Me?" gasped Freeda. "You're disassembling me?"

"You're disassembling Freeda?" said Melvin.

"Melvin!" said Phil. "Don't make me invoke Paragraph H, Nipping Probable Disloyalty in the Bud! Does anyone have a problem with this, other than Melvin? If so, please step forward. And please don't think I will necessarily consider it Disloyal for you to publicly contradict me at this critical national destiny hour. I mean, I probably will, but if you reference Paragraph N, The President's Incredible Mercy, you will see that I, and I alone, reserve the right to be as merciful as I choose about cases of Probable Disloyalty."

No one stepped forward.

"So everyone is fine with this?" said Phil. "Except Melvin?"

"No, I'm fine with it," said Melvin, a little frantically. "I'm totally fine with it."

Freeda did not kneel with her primary connecting parts easily accessible, but stood up straight, thinking of Gertrude, while the Special Friends trimmed back her Sternum Foliage, then removed her Personal Boundary Sensor and her Hat-Holding Pin System and her bulbous Left Foot.

Soon Jimmy was down to the last step, which involved removing Freeda's third arm, which flailed around frantically, as if trying to put out a fire on Jimmy's chest.

"INSURRECTION NIPPED IN BUD!" shouted the first little man.

"PREZ DOES WHAT PREZ MUST DO!" shouted the second.

"What a sad thing, that Freeda should prove to be a traitor!" Phil said. "Well, let this be a lesson to all! A lesson that the disgusting traits that make those Inner Hornerites so disgusting, such as Disloyalty, such as undermining one's leaders via constant questioning, can even take root in us Outer Hornerites. I wouldn't be surprised if some of us didn't start getting smaller and doing mathematical proofs. We'll have to watch for that. We'll have to be vigilant. Jimmy, Vance, please help

Freeda remind us to be vigilant, by constructing an attractive yet sobering display of the components of Freeda, so people can witness Freeda's components, and thus learn from them! What a wonderful thing for Freeda, to be so very educational! In this way, her life will not have been a total waste!"

So the Special Friends made a display of Freeda's parts, by stringing some from trees and setting others on rocks, placing, near each, per Phil, a sign reading: "Loyalty—It's Super!"

Then, almost as an afterthought, Phil nodded to Jimmy, who plucked Old Gus out of the Peace-Encouraging Enclosure and disassembled him, which went very quickly, Old Gus being so frail, brittle, and greaseless.

"PROGRESS CONTINUES APACE!" shouted the second little man.

"TOTAL VICTORY IN SIGHT!" shouted the third.

A great high-pitched wailing now sounded from Inner Horner.

It may have been this that caused Phil's rack to spasm.

Oh shoot, wow, Phil thought, that really hurts.

He had only got this same spasming sensational once before in his life, and that had been the worse, due to, just after that, his speech would began suffering.

Darn, Phil thought. It are happening now, somewhat slight.

He'd better hurry, get this Phase III wropped up, so he could go homer and find that stupid brawn, and remont it.

"That one," Phil gasped, indicating Curtis, and Jimmy yanked Curtis out of the Peace-Encouraging Enclosure, and Jimmy unlatched Curtis's Lower Half, and Vance unbraided the nine tightly braided ropes that constituted Curtis's Upper Half, and Jimmy removed the three bolts joining Curtis's perfectly round head full of thick wavy hair to his Neck Platform, and soon Curtis had been reduced to a twitching pile of parts oozing hydraulic fluid.

At that moment, Dale, Citizen #9 from Greater Keller, burst out from behind the Outer Horner Cafe and sprinted off towards Greater Keller, his shock and disgust at all he had seen causing him to inscribe what was, for him, a remarkably linear path.

"What the heck was that?" said Melvin.

"It sure looked weird," said Leon.

"And it sure ran funny," said Larry.

The truth was, relative to the Inner and Outer Hornerites, the Greater Kellerites did look weird. They had no mechanical or botanical parts, and were tall and whippet-like and stood permanently leaning off to one side as if going around a bend, which, normally, they were.

They were also, it should be mentioned, huge: approximately three times the height of the Special Friends, with significantly less body fat. And longer legs. Their legs were long and lean from constant walking, and they never got tired, and their faces were slightly beveled and aerodynamic, and so, once you got them going, they were incredibly fast runners.

Dale, the fastest of all, reached Greater Keller just six minutes after he left the Border Area.

Nine minutes after Dale left the Border Area, the nation of Greater Keller, coffee cups clinking nervously against their saucers, listened as Dale concluded his report.

"Cliff, how are we doing?" President Rick tersely asked the National Enjoyment Assessor.

"Well, we've been better, sir," said Cliff. "Although our coffee cups are full and we have, on average, four cookies remaining on our plates, the National Life Enjoyment Index Score has dropped to an alarming Three out of Ten. I would attribute this to anxiety associated with Dale's report. In fact, Mr. President, knowing our people as I do, I foresee continued significant downturns in the NLEIS, if we do not in some way address Dale's findings."

"People will mope and feel guilty?" said President Rick.

"I'm afraid so," said Cliff.

"Our coffee will not taste as good?" said President Rick. "When regarding a beautiful vista or hearing a delightful bon mot, our hearts will not be as uplifted, due to we will be thinking of those people far away who need our help?"

"Basically, yes," said Cliff.

"Maybe we should send out an Expeditionary Force," said the First Daughter.

"Oh, gosh, I don't know," said President Rick. "I mean, if this new President is as bad as Dale says, isn't it possible that he might do something bad to our Expeditionary Force? And therefore, wouldn't it be better to keep everybody safe at home? That sounds much more Enjoyable to me."

"Sir, the nation is tense," said Cliff gravely. "It is asking itself how it can possibly stand idly by drinking gourmet coffee when an entire race is about to be disassembled. It wants to Enjoy, yes, but feels it will not be able to fully Enjoy until some sort of closure is reached."

"I'm just really torn about this," said President Rick. "If some of us get hurt, the NLEIS could easily drop below Three. It could even conceivably go into negative numbers."

"We could Suffer," said Lenore.

"We could Suffer, exactly," said President Rick.

"On the other hand," said the First Daughter, "if these people are as bad as Dale says, they could come here next."

"Talk about Suffering," said Kevin.

"They could destroy our coffee cart," said the First Lady.

"They could disassemble us," said Kelli.

"Sir," Cliff whispered urgently. "The NLEIS is dropping like a stone."

"Dang," said President Rick, who had been looking forward to that evening, when he planned on passing around some surprise éclairs and challenging his nation to write a collective national sonnet on the pleasurable sensation of eating an éclair while watching a sunset.

But President Rick knew his people, and knew that the only sonnets they would be able to write now would be sad guilt-racked sonnets, no matter how many éclairs he fed them.

So President Rick ordered Elroy, Citizen #6, the National Coffeemaker, to brew five thermoses of coffee, and had Dale lead a brief preliminary training hike into Outer Horner, during which Dale demonstrated various techniques he had found useful for running in a straight line.

Then the nation of Greater Keller sprinted into Outer Horner, commenting, as was their national habit, on the beauty of the landscape through which they were passing, but in uncharacteristically terse, joyless voices.

*   *   *

"All of them, sir?" Jimmy the Special Friend was saying at that very moment. "Even the ladies?"

"Even the kid?" said Vance.

"I do not see any lady or kids!" shouted Phil. "I only see some curvier Inner Hornerites with longer hair, and one smaller Inner Hornerite with two freakish brains! With Inner Hornerites there is no lady, there is no kid, there are only evil, which must be dealt with harsh, before it spread! Hurry, boys! Seize all remaining national asset, lift said national asses out from the Peace-Encouraging Enclosure plonto!"

So Jimmy plucked Carol and Elmer out of the Peace-Encouraging Enclosure, and Vance plucked Wanda and Little Andy out of the Peace-Encouraging Enclosure, and the entire remaining population of the once-great land of Inner Horner found itself suddenly suspended in the air, legs flailing, seconds from total extinction.

Which was when the Expeditionary Force of the Nation of Greater Keller arrived at the Border Area in five colossal, parallel, dust-raising arcs.

"What in the world?" said President Rick.

"Boys," Phil shouted frantically. "Arrest this invaderment!"

The Special Friends had never in their lives seen anyone bigger than themselves. Suddenly they nostalgically remembered their previous careers as Mud-Consistency Testing Associates. Those were the good old days, when the worst thing that ever happened to them was that occasionally Edna inadvertently left them out in the yard all night, covered in mud.

"SPECIAL FRIENDS FLEE BORDER AREA!" shouted the first little man.

"STRIPPING OFF BIG RED SHIRTS, THEY RUN LIKE WIND!" shouted the second.

"ALREADY THEY ARE OUT OF SIGHT!" shouted the third.

"PRESIDENT PHIL SPEECHLESS WITH HANGING-OPEN MOUTH AND LOOK OF TOTAL SHOCK ON FACE!" shouted the second.

"ANXIOUS NATION AWAITS PRESIDENTIAL STATEMENT!" shouted the third.

Actually, Phil felt, he wasn't feeling all that well. He was feeling totally devanced in terms of how good he could think. Where was that stupid brain? Where dud he left it? That thing had been offen a long time. No wonder no salvation thoughts were come winging out of him. He wanted to communerate to these idiotic tall circle-walking invaders they couldn't know how it was like, forced to live close to a national of inhuman puny coveting your wide open, claiming to be just as human, giving those hostility look just because you lived in a spacious total bounty of righteous plenty. Only suddenly he couldn't seem to speak so super.

Phil's legs gave out, and he sat on the ground near the Peace-Encouraging Enclosure.

"Sir?" said Larry. "Are you okay?"

It could not end this way, it could not end in any way but total triumph redemption of his dream of upward conquest, thereby him, Phil, in gold chair, and all the lessers, lying stretched out at his trenchant feet, citing his blessed nameplate.

"Cruel freight," he mumbled. "Working crosswise to my bold national, fate interdicted my glorious, and due to nefarious, all grand uplift purposes crash down, flags droop, crowds go home."

Then the weight of his brainless rack proved too much, and he slumped over, snagging his rack in the barbed wire of the Peace-Encouraging Enclosure.

A final spark flew out of his nosehole, and he was still.

A great silence fell across the Border Area.

"Mistakes were made," said Larry.

"Excesses were committed," said Leon.

"Let's get those poor people out of that cage, shall we?" said President Rick. "That doesn't look very Enjoyable."

Dale, Citizen #9, with the help of Kelli, Citizen #7, tore down the Peace-Encouraging Enclosure, and the nation of Inner Horner stumbled out.

"Our advice, to all of you people, is Enjoy!" said President Rick. "Life is full of beauty. Why fight? Why hate?

Learn to Enjoy, and you will have no need to fight, and no desire to! Love life, walk in a circle, learn to enjoy coffee! Will you do that? Will you promise to try that?"

The Inner Hornerites looked blankly at President Rick.

"Well, we have to be going!" said President Rick. "I'm sure you folks will figure everything out!"

And the Greater Kellerites started home in a loping victorious arc, their National Enjoyment Level an astonishing 9.8 out of Ten, due to their pride in their recent heroism and their anticipation of the many days of Enjoyable storytelling that lay ahead.

"I told Phil this would happen," said the mirror-faced Advisor.

"So did I," said the smiley Advisor.

"I said to him, Phil, honestly, who do you think you are, let's not get too big for our britches," said the mirror-faced Advisor.

"I think we all said that," said the mere mouth.

"HOW WAS NATION SO EASILY DUPED?" shouted the first little man.

"WHY DID NATION IGNORE REPEATED WARNINGS BY MEDIA?" shouted the second.

"NERVOUS-LOOKING ADVISORS LEAVE AREA AT FAST WALK!" shouted the third.

"MAJOR MEDIA FIGURES BRAVELY FOLLOW

STRANGE EXODUS FROM BORDER AREA, DETERMINED TO SEE WHAT IS UP WITH THAT!" shouted the first.

And the Advisors and media men left the Border Area, the Advisors discussing strategies for reminding the former President of how constantly loyal they had been to him, the media men feverishly whispering potential headlines out their rear-mouths.

The Inner Hornerites (Elmer, Carol, Little Andy, and Wanda), suddenly realizing they now outnumbered the Outer Hornerites (Leon, Larry, and Melvin), fell upon the Outer Hornerites with all the fury of a people who, naked and starving, had been imprisoned for days on end, in a cage, on the brink of extinction. Soon from out of the rising cloud of dust there flew a cotter pin (Melvin's) and a Temperature Gauge (Leon's), and Larry's Frontal Hairpiece, and several unidentified Teeth Plates, and suddenly it was the nation of Outer Horner, inside the cloud of dust, that found itself on the brink of extinction.

Which was when, in the sky above the Border Area, there appeared a hand so massive that its golden ring could easily have encircled the entire Border Area. Across its wrist ran a vast flower garden, one of its three fingers was mechanical, in its palm was what appeared to be a shimmering blue lake.

The Outer Hornerites and Inner Hornerites had all thought about the Creator, and talked about the Creator, and some of them had even prayed to the Creator, but none of them had ever dreamed the Creator was so big.

The fighting stopped, the dust cloud settled, the nations of Inner and Outer Horner stared up, wide-eyed and open-mouthed.

Then a second hand descended, with a vegetable garden running across the wrist, and two mechanical fingers, and a frozen lake in its palm, holding a spray can, and the Creator's left hand sprayed the Border Area, and the Outer and Inner Hornerites fell instantly asleep.

The two hands, working together, gently disassembled the Outer Hornerites.

Then they gently disassembled the Inner Hornerites.

Using the Inner and Outer Horner parts, they rapidly constructed fifteen entirely new little people.

The only parts they didn't use were Phil's parts. Phil's brain (retrieved from under his couch, covered in chip-crumbs and lint, giving off the hissing noise a Type C brain makes when off-gassing) they dropped into the stream, where several of the new fish, mistaking it for a misshapen fallen apple, began eating it. Phil's body, they mounted on a platform, after first spray-painting it black and mounting a plaque beneath it.

"PHIL," the plaque read. "MONSTER."

Then the massive hands lifted the new people up to a pair of giant indescribable lips and whispered, in a fundamentally untranslatable Creator-language, something that meant, approximately: THIS TIME, BE KIND TO ONE ANOTHER. REMEMBER: EACH OF YOU WANTS TO BE HAPPY. AND I WANT YOU TO. EACH OF YOU WANTS TO LIVE FREE FROM FEAR. AND I WANT YOU TO. EACH OF YOU ARE SECRETLY AFRAID YOU ARE NOT GOOD ENOUGH. BUT YOU ARE, TRUST ME, YOU ARE.

Then the left hand picked up the green string that constituted the boundary of the Short-Term Residency Zone, and the right hand picked up the red string that constituted the Inner Horner border, and the left hand took away the remnants of the Peace-Encouraging Enclosure, while the right hand planted a sign reading: "Welcome to New Horner."

Then the hands did that dusting-off thing hands do when they've just finished a difficult piece of work, and withdrew, majestically, through a large white cloud.

Soon the fifteen new people woke up, stretching and yawning. Where the heck were they? And who the heck were they? They felt sort of sore. Apparently, they concluded, by looking at the sign, they were New Hornerites, and lived in New Horner. Apparently, they concluded, reading the little name-tags around their necks, they each had a name.

They were, they all agreed, just amazingly hungry.

On the way to a nearby apple tree, they passed a hulking black mess on a platform.

"What is that thing?" said Gil.

"It's a Phil," said Clive.

"What is a Phil?" said Sally.

"A monster," said Leona.

"Apparently," said Fritz.

"Or maybe Monster was his last name?" said Gil. "You know: Phil Monster. Like: Hi, I'm Phil Monster? It's not entirely clear from the syntax."

"Whatever," said Sally. "Let's go eat."

Leona looked at Gil. *Syntax?* What the heck kind of word was that? What was Gil, some kind of big-shot? She hated big-shots, she suddenly realized. She'd have to watch Gil. She'd talk to Sally about it. Sally didn't seem like a big-shot. Sally seemed sensible and moral and down to earth. Sally, like Leona, was compressed and ball-shaped, unlike the freakishly elongated Gil.

As the months went by, the New Hornerites took to avoiding The Phil. Although nobody could exactly say why, The Phil gave them the creeps. Soon the path bowed out around it, weeds overtook it, and all that could be seen of The Phil was the tip of Phil's rack, which stuck out of the weeds like a bad flagpole. Animals burrowed in The Phil, birds nested there, balls accumulated there because the New Horner kids were too scared to retrieve them.

And that is where Phil is today: hidden in a thicket of weeds, not loved, not hated, just forgotten, rusting/rotting, with even the sign that proclaims his name fading away.

Except sometimes Leona comes to visit. She does not find The Phil monstrous, but strangely beautiful, and sometimes sits in the thicket for hours, dreaming, for reasons she can't quite explain, of a better world, run by humble, compressed, ball-shaped people, like her and Sally, who speak, when they speak at all, in short sentences, of their simple heroic dreams.

acknowledgments

The author wishes to thank the Lannan Foundation, the Syracuse University College of Arts and Sciences, and his colleagues and students in the Syracuse Creative Writing Program, for their generous support during the writing of this book.

GEORGE SAUNDERS

'One of the geniuses of 21st century fiction'
Guardian

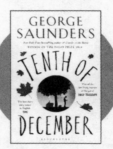

'It would be an understatement
to call this novel an
extraordinary tour de force'
Sunday Times

'The best book you'll
read this year'
New York Times

'Not since Twain has America
produced a satirist this funny'
Zadie Smith

'Surreal
and puncturing'
Margaret Atwood

'Just the kind of stories
we need to get us through
these times'
Thomas Pynchon

BLOOMSBURY

www.bloomsbury.com/author/george-saunders